Ice Monarch

They have said...

Michèle Laframboise

Ice Monarch

Echofictions

Echovisions Collection

Ice Monarch©Copyright 2018 Michèle Laframboise

Original publication in Abyss&Apex 67 June 2018

Cover design by Echofictions
Cover pictures of ice and butterfly © Shutterstock
Author portrait © Gilles Gagnon
Interior illustrations by the author

This book published by : Echofictions
Mississauga, Ontario

www.echofictions.com

ISBN 978-1-988339-60-3 (print)

Table of Contents

For Joël Champetier

who took flight too soon

Ice Monarch

WINGS OUTSTRETCHED, I chased my shadow across a floating desert crossed by a few polar bears and the mobile palaces of the Ice Lords. What was left of me barely registered the cold.

The white bears felt as lost here as they were before we took pity on them. Although synthetic ice gave purchase for their paws, lack of preys confined them to the edges of the North Pole. I mulled over the irony: the old Greeks had originally named this ephemeral continent *Arctos* — land of the bear.

With my enhanced vision, I could make out the thin cracks running along the edges of the joined-up floes, forming a white jigsaw puzzle.

Somewhere on this giant puzzle, was my lifeline, my base. After my long peregrinations, my inner compass pulled me toward it like a magnet.

*

SYNTHETIC ICE HAD SEEMED like a good idea at the time.

Pale areas reflected sunlight back in space; dark areas absorbed the heat. Covering the pole with a white polymer sheet would augment the Earth's albedo and curb global warming.

The construction of this arctic jigsaw took twelve years. Hundreds of ships — freighters, converted whalers, passenger ferries, even luxury yatches from bankrupt CEO — sailed north, their holds full of liquid polymer.

First, workers sprayed a rectangular segment of sea with polyurethane foam. The foam solidified as it touched water, its trapped air bubbles ensuring buoyancy. Next, additives hardened the upper surface. The result was a nice patch of synthetic ice, serrated edges ready to fuse with another patch. A new segment of sea was marked out and the process began anew.

Alas, political quarrels about cost-sharing erupted among the powers. Funding channels closed down before the new ice barely covered four million square kilometers.

Tossed around by sea currents, this big chunk of polymer bumped with clockwork regularity against the coasts of Greenland, Siberia, Alaska and Canada.

*

A DARK CIRCLE appeared ahead of me. Free water areas were intended to give marine life a chance to survive. As no seal could dig fishing holes through hard polymer, the hapless mammals had to surface in the designated oasis.

A brown areola of dried excrements, bones and blood smeared the edge. Orcas and polar bears had soon adapted to the new conditions. The oasis turned into killing zones.

Two kilometers past the open water trap, I spotted a dark speck on the whiteness. Not a lonely seal. This speck moved so fast no polar bear could hope to make a meal with it.

I focussed my vision.

The dark blur resolved into the fugitive servant. His torso was bent forward as if praying non existent gods, to keep off the cold. His mechanical spider legs threw up chips of polyurethane mixed with some real ice in his wake. His run created an almost artistic pattern of traces on the gleaming surface.

The man was trying to reach a competitor's mobile palace. Few were in range, since the thirty or thirty one surviving palaces were scattered over four million square kilometers of synthetic ice. The freezing cold or his failing batteries would soon kill him.

I took another look. The servant was clutching a black container to his heart. A stolen reserve battery, no doubt.

So his escape had been more well-planned than most. He wore layers of fabrics over his butler vest. A mask and goggles covered most of his face, giving no inkling of his age. He was male of course, as all our modified spider servants were. I computed the odds again. The extra battery would gave him a faint chance to reach another Ice Lord's palace.

His determination filled me with admiration, mixed with sadness. I knew my duty. My employers would want the spider servant's bio-implants back.

I recorded his speed and direction, then turned toward my base.

*

A CONGREGATION of shiny domes bubbled up over the milky horizon. The palace trundled forward on its array of huge wheels.

I soared over the main dome. Heirs to the last financial empires, the Ice Lords lived in self-contained environments, their whims catered to by an army of servants. A coterie of scientists and doctors worked around the clock to extend their life spans.

Today, the thirty or so mobile palaces formed the last advanced civilization left on Earth.

I spiraled down toward a green secondary dome. Beneath the clear plastic, a greenhouse blossomed. My life-line jutted out from the top, a long pole merging with the dome's cover. I bent my wings to slow my dscent. The pole came to me, too fast. I clutched the shaft with my median arms, inertia making the rest of me swirling around it.

At last, my wings draped themselves over the dome, plunging the greenhouse in shade.

Servants stopped watering the orchard to look up. Few of them had kept their human form. Like me, they were modified and remodeled to add a few decades to their life expectancy.

I unfurled my antennas to jack into the pole's receptor port. Pictures from the rest of the planet flowed into the Lord's datanet.

Meanwhile, my lifeline looked after me, other ports opening, bottle green caterpillars spreading essential oils on my wings to keep them flexible, filling up my brain's nutrient reserves, calibrating my sensors: thermometer, altimeter, anemometer... the works.

Children —fully human, those— ran darting to and fro around the servant's spidery legs. The sons and daughters of the Ice Lords were the sole palace denizens able to reproduce.

They, too, lifted up their eyes. My visits were infrequent occurrences. A girl with pale green hair waved at me. Surrounded all her life by cyborgs, she showed no fear of my form : a black torso, four forearms to manipulate delicate instruments or grasp a pole, two powerful grasshopper legs to propel me towards the sky.

And my best feature, in the younger children's eyes: two immense wings, their vibrant orange striated with black lines. Soft as synthetic silk, they could resist the strong convection winds of mountain ranges and withstand the highest shearing stresses. You could suspend a five-ton truck from each of my wingtips without tearing them apart.

Some parts of me retained their original form: the mold encasing my brain and spinal cord was sculpted into a human face, with large eyes. A small family of cameras and sensors lining my ocular globes gave me an eagle's sharpness of vision. I could perceive the light range from ultraviolet to infrared. Perched atop a mountain, I could spot an ant scurrying on the floor of the valley.

Or a runaway servant.

Upon landing, my first act had been to transmit the coordinates of the fugitive. The Lords could order a crew sent to recover him. Of course, his fate after an escape attemps would not be desirable. The Lords would have to punish him. After being stripped from his bioimplants, the servant could be devolved into a waste sorting cyborg. Locked down in the palace's basement, he would never see the sky again.

While the caterpillars oiled my wings, I saw a slot opening on a smaller, opaque dome. A slim dark pencil shot off from it. Lacking ears, I did not hear its launch. It gathered height and speed, then arrowed off.

So.

My Lords had decided to do without the servant's costly bioimplants after all. Maybe sending a recovery crew at this distance was not cost-effective. Maybe they feared a leak of industrial secrets to competing cities. Or they needed to set a clear example for the other servants.

Under the darkening sky, the tiny flash of a faraway detonation winked.

*

WHEN I TRANSFORMED into a monarch, it was with my eyes open.

I lost my eyes, of course. But my change gave me more than a simple life extension. Instead of clinging to a withering body, I drank the sun's energy captured by my silky wings. My emotions were toned down by the absence of a blood circulation system and endocrine glands. However, my brain remained intact, mind sharp as a scalpel. I had made the good choice, going through the exit door.

I detected movement in the greenhouse. The children had scattered.

An Ice Lord was observing me. His fibrous protein hair fell in a long turquoise mane, his rejuvenated body encased in a skin-tight garment. I did not know his actual age. Was he an adult of the present generation, or an ancestor sitting beside me on a UN committee? Some names have flown out of my brain when I became a butterfly.

A flick of his well-manicured hand told me to get back to the job that justified my prolonged existence. I unplugged myself from the mast, my antennae folding inside their grooves. All my indicators were in the green.

I bent my knees and leaped into an endless indigo.

I climbed to the troposphere's limit. My lungs, if I still had them, would have starved for oxygen.

*

NIGHT AND DAY, I fluttered, a heartless, lungless butterfly.

At 148 years of age, I had achieved twice the life expectancy predicted at my birth. I seldom thought of my previous life.

Long ago, I led rallies, attended Climate Change Symposiums, took part in the laying of the first puzzle pieces of the artificial ice. Meanwhile, like an ice cube dropped in a glass of water, run-off from melting glaciers had chilled the local weather.

"What global warming?" industrialists asked, laughing out loud.

Worse, the warming sea stopped the Gulf Stream current. Paris, London and most European capitals experimented the harsh winters that Canadians came to miss. Oil kings dug in their deep pockets to wash their hands off this "natural perturbation cycle." They hired hackers and agents-provocateurs to disrupt and discredit the green organizations.

Funding to the North Pole puzzle project dried up.

I jumped from one precarious contract to the next. I learned to code in the new protocols. My family eventually scattered, but a survival instinct — or sheer cussedness — preserved me.

I could always sense which way the wind blew – towards the money. Heading a small army of public-relation experts, I joined the winning side.

As the climate warnings sank to the bottom of the public opinion pond, my bosses returned to their usual pastimes: concentrating capital, abolishing workers' standards, automating productivity.

Sheltered under their wing, I coded fresh gems of robotic science.

*

JUST WHEN THE LAST DROP of the Himalayan glaciers disappeared into the dried-up clay of the Indus River, the thawing permafrost released millions of tons of methane gas.

This time, the mercury climbed up, all over the planet.

The full blown greenhouse effect shifted all climatic zones up north. Deserts pushed up the tropical zones while squeezing the equatorial band into a narrow ribbon.

The colorful autumns of the temperate regions replaced the taiga.

The treeless tundra disappeared, never to be seen again.

Civil war and political assassinations ruined nations. Cities became concrete wastelands. Facing this calamity, the happy few dug again in their deep pockets, their Swiss bank accounts.

Most had their exit door ready.

A few opted for a lunar hotel ticket, some others for a mansion in the new metropolises of Siberia and Alaska. The North Pole beckoned, as the newly thawed Antarctica had been annexed by China.

The Ice Lords cities rolled on.

By that time, long past retirement age, I cast my lot with the last oil magnate. I supervised the building of his rolling palace. I took some time away to find my family and invite Eliane and her children to come with me. She refused.

So I continued to please and amuse, to optimize and manage. When my body, worn out past all hope of recovery, began its final decline, I managed one last leap.

The ecologist became a butterfly.

*

THE OCEAN REMAINED THE SAME, a great table alive with green and turquoise eddies. The Mexican coast loomed ahead, broken in pink and grey fractals.

The jagged Himalaya peaks looked like old teeth with some snow jammed in the cracks. I sailed over the flooded San Andreas fault, across the mouths of sleeping volcanoes, over falls so high that water evaporated before it could reach the ground. I can recall the round blue eye of the Sahara, the Richat Structure in Mauritania, a geological wonder visible from space...

The feeling of wonder kept me going on.

I never slept. At night, through my infrared sensors, jungle plants screamed out their will to live in alien violets and reds. My artificial eyes drank those landscapes until bliss juice soaked my soul.

*

As A CHILD, I spent hours curled up in the library, musing over breathtaking landscapes seen from the sky. I watched TV documentaries about migratory birds.

Most of all, monarch butterflies fascinated me. I remember my father driving me to the Niagara Conservatory, the two of us walking amidst thousands of fluttering orange sparks.

One landed on my shoulder... and a sudden joy fizzed up and sparked under my cranium.

Bliss juice, my father would say, smiling.

*

ADULT MONARCHS did not live more than two months. But when fall came, the latest generation forgot to die. Males and females flew south, a journey of four thousand kilometers. Belying their frail appearance, monarchs rode the air currents, soaring even higher than migratory birds.

I had flown over the monarch's wintering home in California and Mexico, arid hills. Each insect weighed less than half a gram, but their numbers bent the cypress and pine branches, covering them with shivering orange fur.

After the spring mating, the females crept up north, step by fluttering step, laying eggs en route. From those eggs, sprang a new generation that would continue the journey. Sometimes, I encountered those long orange undulations. Stirred by nostalgia, I would keep my wings still to avoid shredding my smaller counterparts.

Like them, I had forgotten to die.

One other thing to remember about monarchs: caterpillars fed on the latex-like sap of milkweed plants, a deeply toxic compound. The butterfly's flesh inherited the poison.

Birds left them alone.

*

I LET THE WINDS carry me over Europe's scars, dead cities with little rectangles of razed bungalows and large squares of collapsed supermarkets. Kilometers of empty shelves, their abundance forgotten. Murderous fights among scavenger groups also provided edifying pictures for the domes' dwellers.

The countryside was derelict fields overgrown with arid-zone grasses, asphalt roads vanished under layers of drift-dirt. A green patch on the ground signaled an orchard, a fortified farm near a deep-water well. Determined farmers toiled, always checking over their shoulders for pillagers.

The old capitals parliaments, silent and empty. My infrared sensors revealed burgeoning rodent populations.

Somewhere, under those ruins, lay the bones of my daughter.

I often thought about Eliane as I sailed over the heaps of shattered brick and moldering concrete. I recalled her face and the faces of her children, in their pitiful commune, as I left them to catch the corporate shuttle.

Eliane had refused to follow me through the exit door. She was a rebel. She joined other marginal artists and poets, idealists without future. For a long time, I kept the poetry book that she sent me.

Two months before my final metamorphosis, I learned that Eliane, my sweet light, had been snuffed out, erased by premature old age and disease.

*

FIERY EMERALD WINGS dashed from the sky. Another butterfly.

Our absence of vocal chords made talking impossible. No mikes, no loudspeakers. Our equipment only served for transmitting our harvest of pictures.

We wrote words on the clouds, in cursive script.

His name was Joshua.

Mine was Dominique.

Joshua had flown eight years for the Mutual-Omale, another ice palace. He was already fed up with his borrowed body. This body that was — I knew it long before signing my own agreement — the last that we would inhabit.

In theory, my masters could transfer my brain and spinal cord into a biological vat-grown body. In practice, the high failure rate and the few available resources limited the application of this procedure, especially on a mere servant.

Before ending his life, Joshua wanted to see his country of birth, the Netherlands. I mentioned the cracked dams, the roads lying under four meters of water. He told me about the fishermen reclaiming the territory, their villages raised on stilts forming a string of islands.

I wrote: *it won't last.*

He signalled: *we'll see.*

*

A CHAOTIC LANDSCAPE spread beneath me, disputed by dozens of warlords. Columns of refugees faded into the dim horizon. More refugees lined up outside green tents at the desert's edge. The rare relief organizations had to kowtow to warlords' whims.

I recorded all this for the edification of the domes' children. The Ice Lords weren't cut off from the world. Their tank-factories ponderously rolled across ravaged lands. When one of these mastodons detected a deposit, it stopped and drilled into the soil. Factories also harvested trees and other resources for the domes. Automated barges conveyed the goods to the ice-field harbor.

Sometimes, people were already onsite, trying to live off the land. If they interfered with the mobile factories, the Ice Lords would engage a local warlord's militia. I had recorded these "pacifying" events. My employers made sure they were getting what they paid for.

I just had to jack in the factory's antenna to send my own harvest. Of course, for my vital maintenance, I had to return to my masters' abode.

A flurry of movements alerted my sensors. I fine-tuned my telescopic vision.

Barely distinct from the arid earth, two bearded men trained their still-functioning guns on me. Black-garbed women ran from a well and dashed into a stone keep. In this mosaic of carpet-sized states dominated by warlords, anything in the sky was a threat.

The bullets reaching my altitude had lost so much kinetic energy that they bounced off my shell like soft grapes.

Even if I descended lower, my butterfly body was next to invulnerable. A lucky shot from an elephant gun could probably section off my wing tie, but for that to happen, I would have to fly on my back.

A ground-to-air cannon?

There were not enough left in working order to worry me.

*

SOMEWHERE over what had once been Turkey, an oval shape caught my eye.

Curious, I sailed closer. A two-way transmitter dangled from a large balloon. Until now, I had only encountered the antennas of the Ice Lords palaces and their rolling plants. The transparent top of the balloon let the sun warm the air inside. The underside was painted a bright azure blue.

Downward, crops sculpted the mountainsides, slanting into a narrow valley dotted with round huts and tents.

An independent agrarian society had nestled in the mountains, a mere bird flight from the nearest warlord's keep. Amazed, I observed four or five hundred people going about their tasks, tilling the soil, cleaning solar captors. I tightened my focus to discover a woman reading an actual book salvaged from some library.

There was something different about those crops. The villagers grew those in burlap bags filled with dirt, the plants poking their green heads through the holes — moveable crops, a smart innovation. They could pack up and move quickly. Those resourceful people would not hinder the tank-factories.

I started recording.

Such good news needed to be relayed to my employers. Moreover, the balloon suggested that there might be similar villages dotting the mountains. I banked in a long curve and struck out in the direction of the mobile factory.

When I had all I needed, I located the nearest rolling mine, only a short flight away. I landed on its mast, antennae unrolling and plugging into the receptor. A moment later, my images would appear on a screen far to the north.

*

Having nothing better to do with my days, I went back to the hidden village.

My wings drinking the sun, I floated lazily over their toiling days, too high to be seen. As I spied on them, I was surprised to feel an echo of my father's bliss juice stirring in me.

Life in this *Shangri-La* did not look easy. Under their large straw hats, I could not see their faces. Only their hands were visible to my enhanced eyes: soft-skinned children's hands on the green shoots, browned fingers of the youths tending the crops, wrinkled hands of old men and women who would probably die clutching their work tools.

I soon identified individuals: the chief under a bright red hat, two medics, a once-scarlet crescent paling on their dirty blouses, an older woman who took care of the books and of teaching the next generation. Once, she took off her hat to wipe sweat from its rim. The face bore an uncanny likeness to Eliane. It occurred to me that she might be one of my own grandchildren; she looked about the right age.

Some of the people wore the green of cooperants, or their rough equivalents. They attended to the balloon, recharged the solar batteries and wore cellular phones on their belts. Judging by the heat signals from their tent, I surmised they might use other surviving technologies, like old computers.

I had not flown long before, at the end of a canyon, a line of black dots drew my attention. I focused in and made out trucks, uniforms, heavy machine guns. I consulted my GPS. Their path was clear. They needed only to continue a mere hundred kilometers of bad roads twisting in the mountains.

They would reach *Shangri-La* tomorrow.

The local warlords resented my unreachable employers, but a tip about a dissident village had prodded them to action.

I had plenty of time to get to get back in time to record hell and destruction falling upon the villagers. The Ice Lords liked to show such images to their servants, to remind them how lucky they were.

*

As I flew toward the factory, I replayed the image of the woman's face. It was, of course, as clear and perfect as my advanced systems permitted. I tried to call up Eliane's face, and those of her brown-haired children. With less success. Still, there was a resemblance, wasn't there?

I looked down at the landscape unrolling beneath me and tried to summon some bliss juice. But it wouldn't come. This time the memory of Eliane's face came unbidden, the hurt in her eyes when last I'd seen them, the children's lack of understanding. I had chosen my path. There was no going back... I had not even turned as I walked away.

Why is Grampa leaving us? The smallest girl had said behind me.

Something within me tipped, a bowl of dark bitter juice spilling out. Then I was frantically looking for another exit door.

Later, I attached myself to the mine's mast, plugging my antennas to the receptor. I discharged my recent harvest: pictures of their toiling days, heat signature of their surviving computers, postcard views of the surrounding mountains, and, buried deep inside those infos... milkweed juice.

*

BACK ABOVE THE VILLAGE, I folded my wings and plummeted down.

People in the fields stopped what they were doing. They may have screamed: the medics and cooperants came out from their shelter. The woman who looked like Eliane had been reading to some little ones; she shepherded them behind her.

I knew what they were seeing, dropping out of the sky with tent-sized orange wings. A giant Monarch butterfly, wearing a human face.

I have never touched down on hard ground. My grasshopper hind legs absorbed the shock.

Absence.

Return.

My fainting spell had lasted 14.02 seconds. The impact must have shaken my brain in its nutrient soup. Fortunately, I lacked the nerve endings to feel pain. Another sensor told me that hands — children's hands — were feeling my dusty wings.

My eyes came back on line to a blinding light. I adjusted the luminosity. A circle of heads, bearded or smooth, stood out against the sky.

Worry lined those faces, the one under the red hat being the most creased. The one that reminded me of Eliane moved her lips, but I could not answer her. My tongue, my palate, my larynx... all gone.

But I could still communicate.

My antennas rolled out of their creases, striking fear in the children. I found the frequency linking the balloon's transmitter to their cell phones. I transmitted pictures of the trucks and weapons, their map position, an estimate of their arrival time.

And, while I was at it, I gave them a lot more: the European cities in ruins, the Ice Lords, the polar palaces with their spider servants, the mobile factories.

The chief lifted his red hat and waved it.

His signal sent everyone into feverish action: the shelters were taken down, the balloon pulled to the ground, deflated and folded; the crop-bags were loaded on carts pulled by sturdy bicycles. Two hours later, the whole community was on the move. The children looked back at me from the carts, their eyes still wide with wonder.

But carts left tracks, too visible for trackers armed with guns.

Stupid: I should have thought about it.

My hind legs propelled me into the air. I expended a lot of energy beating my wrinkled and dusty wings. At last, I caught an updraft of warm air. When I was high enough, I recorded the wagon train. Then I superimposed it on another background, tidied up around the edges and other coordinates.

The factory had slightly deviated in its direction while I flew away. I grabbed the mast and uploaded my false trail. Getting back in the sky drained more of my energy reserve. I found the convoy.

A few kilometers farther on, the lead truck came to a fork in the road. Without hesitation, it took the right-hand route. And from then on, kilometer by kilometer, the killers went the wrong way.

*

I GLIDED, SAVING MY STRENGTH, over the tank factory. Its trail of devastation confirmed its course change.

The "milkweed" virus I had injected wouldn't force those great machines to delete their own systems; there were too many built-in safety redundancies. I had written most of the code that governed the rolling factories.

But tampering with its GPS guide was easier, as was getting my factory to spread the news of a colossal new ore deposit. If I'd still had a mouth and throat I could have chuckled at the irony: all over the world, my employers' and their rival's huge land-rapers were rolling toward the nearest sea.

The behemoths would reach the water's edge. They would mindlessly continue towards the ghost deposit, deeper and deeper, until water pressure finally crushed them.

The Ice Lords would attempt to remedy this lemming behavior remotely. It wouldn't work. My "milkweed juice" had seen to that.

They would have to come out in person.

Out in the wreckage of civilization, predators far more deadly than polar bears waited, the warlords' who had until now carried their commands, the angry survivors chased form their homes. Whoever would emerge victorious was no more my concern.

But there would be changes.

*

MY NUTRIENT RESERVES are dropping.

The intranet system of the Ice Lords have recorded my «milkweed juice» upload. Moreover, by helping those families to escape, I have trangressed my non-intervention pact. The doors of their paradise will remain closed.

I could fly to the Antartic continent, knock at the Chinese's door. And get shut down by their ground-air cannons, in working order, those.

I could lose myself in the rarefied altitudes, like Joshua. Plunge into the blue eyes of the sea. Or lie over a mute Parliament's frontispice, wings extended like an orange canopy. Or lock my brain, right now, and let the winds carry me. Plenty of choices.

I shut down my GPS and close my eyes.

Afraid?

Of what?

A butterfly who has lived for 148 years is perfectly able to die in peace.

*

My father holding my hand, we walk on flat stones in the Niagara Butterfly Conservatory, near the famous falls roaring away. A little girl with short brown hair scampers in the grass.

Surrounding us, thousands of monarchs dance from one flower to another, their black-tinged orange wings beating a soft ballet.

I am convinced their tiny hearts are filled with bliss juice.

THE END

Heartfelt Thanks

Already the last page...

If you enjoyed this story, share your impressions
on your favorite platform! This way, you gently
guide more readers towards this author!

Distinctions

Original Publication in Solaris 175

> Winner of the 2010 Solaris Prize for best short-story in French language

Re-Printed in 2012 in Galaxies 18
– Spécial Réchauffement

> Winner of the Special Jury award, Réchauffement 2050 contest

Publication in the double issue of *Supernovia* in 2014

Publication in the online magazine Abyss&Apex in June 2018

Postface

IT'S A BALM FOR THE SOUL and a precious memory to hear the voice of my colleague Joël Champetier tell me that I won the 2010 Solaris Prize for «Ice Monarch», my story submitted to the Solaris competition and published in issue 175 of the magazine.

I became even more proud as when the same Joël, editor of Solaris, called me in 2006 to announce the same happy news for another text, «The flight of the bee» a text that have since morphed into a novel.

Joël was a humble and friendly author who was always encouraging novice writers, me among them. Despite the success around his works, Joël remained very friendly and it was a pleasure to hear him tell funny anecdotes about some SF conferences.

Alas, he left us by a starry night of May 2015. At the preceeding Boreal Congress, too ill to travel onsite, Joël spoke to us through a Skype session (hurrah for technology!)

It is therefore appropriate to dedicate this edition of Ice Monarch for him

*

This dystopian SF story originates in 2009, when a call for SF texts issued by a science journal on the theme of «humanity in one hundred years».

Pulling ideas from my sceince training and my interest in the impacts of global warming, I wrote a text imagining an artificial sea ice. Very soon, having exceeded the limit of words, I continued writing this vision of a future, in an atomized society. It is this expanded version that has been submitted to the Solaris competition.

*

The story does not end there. Selected by Galaxies magazine for its Global Warming 2050 competition, the winning text of the Special Jury Prize was published in 2012 in special Issue 18.

And a Russian translation did appear in the Supernovia science-fiction magazine 45-46, 2014.

*

My own English translation was eventually published in the online magazine Abyss & Apex in June 2018. I am grateful to the publisher Wendy S. Delmater (abyssapexzine.com) who has agreed to publish it.

The English version has undergone some changes from the first French text. I am grateful to author Robert Runte's suggestions that helped flesh out the Monarch's universe with vivid details.

About the Author

WHEN NOT TRYING to initiate first contact with strange flora, Michèle Laframboise juggles her time between drawing comics and crafting stories.

A science-fiction lover since childhood, she has published 17 novels and more than 40 short stories, earning three Auroras and two Solaris awards.

Her works have appeared in *Solaris, Carmilla, Galaxies, Géante Rouge, Brin d'Éternité, Tesseracts, Fiction River, Compelling Science Fiction,* and *Abyss&Apex*. She has been translated into French, Italian and Russian.

Holding degrees in geography and engineering, she uses her scientific background to create worlds filled with humor, invention and wonder.

Official website:
www.michele-laframboise.com

Humoristic blog:

sundayartist.wordpress.com

Publisher's website:
www.echofictions.com

For some news and amusing reading reviews, join Michele's happy band of readers!

http://michele-laframboise.com/fans

Other books by Michèle

Change or die!

Science-fiction / humor / First contact /

Loongunis need constant fluctuations to thrive, while the strange-haired Earthmen hate the endless unstability.

When a sabotage impairs the shift engines of their traveling Box, the enforced immobility might drive all Loongunis mad...unless their translator can work out a solution!

Science fiction adventure at its best, a quirky 7000-word story told by multiple award-winning author Michèle Laframboise.

How to Think inside the Box
978-1-988339-40-5 (print)
978-1-988339-36-8 (epub)

Trapped in the most beautiful place on earth... What's a fearless birder to do?

Humur / mystery / Ornithology

Equipped with her Sibley Guide and trusty binoculars, Amanda Byrd pursues the most elusive winged species. As she explores a beautiful canyon at dawn, Amanda discovers their lift sabotaged, trapping their group at the canyon's bottom.

Who did it, and why?

Our intrepid birdwatcher must find a way out before the sun turns the canyon into a mortal cauldron.

A short and spirited cozy mystery introducing the energetic Lady Byrd, written by Michèle Laframboise, multi-award winner author and amateur ornithologist.

Condor Cliff

ISBN 978-1-988339-08-5 (Print)
ISBN 978-1-988339-02-3 (Epub)
ISBN 978-1-988339-07-8 (Kindle)

You won't forget Malak...

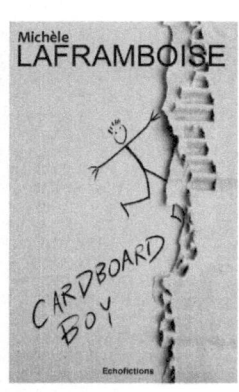

Child Labor/ Humanitarian / Sweatshops

Theo, a dispirited workplace humanitarian, audits a child worker at a cardboard factory, in a port city somewhere in Asia. He is impressed by young Malak's maturity and grit. When that boy, the same age as Theo's own son, disappears, he cannot let it rest. His quest for answers only raises more questions about the traps of structured help and acquired privilege.

An unsettling story quietly told by multiple awards-winning author Michèle Laframboise.

Cardboard Boy

ISBN 978-1-988339-22-1 (Print)
ISBN 978-1-988339-19-1 (epub)
ISBN 978-1-988339-22-1 (Kindle)

More on Echofictions.com

Friends' List

*A story links every reader in a chain of
friendship. Feel free to write your name before
you give this book to someone close.
This is a unique feature of the printed edition!*

_____

_____

_____

_____

_____

_____

_____

_____

_____

Yearning for more Stories?

Michèle Laframboise's full bibliography is enough to whet any reader's appetite! Visit her author site at:
michele-laframboise.com

New stories are brewing up constantly!

To get exclusive offers, curated book reviews, advanced information on events, join Michele's happy band of readers!

(michele-laframboise.com/fans)

As a very busy writer, Michèle won't send mail more often than once every two months.